Rhyme Time

Squeaky Clean

First published in 2006 by
Franklin Watts
338 Euston Road
London
NW1 3BH

Franklin Watts Australia
Hachette Children's Books
Level 17/207 Kent Street
Sydney
NSW 2000

A CIP catalogue record for this book is available
from the British Library.

ISBN 0 7496 6588 2 (hbk)
ISBN 0 7496 6805 9 (pbk)

Series Editor: Jackie Hamley
Series Advisor: Dr Barrie Wade
Series Designer: Peter Scoulding

Printed in China

Squeaky Clean

by Jane Clarke

Illustrated by Anni Axworthy

W
FRANKLIN WATTS
LONDON • SYDNEY

Little Ellie has a scheme

to keep the whole zoo
squeaky clean.

Watch out animals,
big and small!

Here she comes to
squirt you all!

When Ellie turns her
trunk to spray,

three tiny mice are
washed away.

Ellie needs an extra squirt
to blast off Hippo's
crust of dirt.

11

Eek!

She has to shoot
a water jet

to reach the top
of Giraffe's neck.

Even Skunk smells
like a flower

14

after Ellie's power shower.

She's not afraid,
she has no fears
of Crocodile's teeth ...

... or Tiger's ears.

Anaconda's looking grimy,

but Ellie makes him bright
and shiny.

She washes apes
and kangaroos

Eek!

with foamy soap suds
and shampoos.

Now she's scrubbing
Leopard's belly.

But Leopard's never
spotless, Ellie!

And zebras are meant

to be striped,

no matter how hard
they are wiped!

When animals want
to be smelly,
you just can't keep
them clean ...

... poor Ellie.

Now Ellie has a
scheme that's new,

and they're all
happy at the zoo.

Watch out visitors,
big and small!

Eek!

Drop litter and she'll
squirt you all!

31

Leapfrog has been specially designed to fit the requirements of the National Literacy Strategy. It offers real books for beginning readers by top authors and illustrators.

There are 43 Leapfrog stories to choose from:

* hardback